Jolene
The Disability Awareness Chicken

By Karen Finnegan
Copyright Karen Finnegan
Illustrations by Melissa Nastasi

First edition
www.ChickensWithAttitude.com

Hi! My name is Jolene!

I am a baby chicken, called a chick.

I was born on April 30, 2021. I was born the same day as my five brothers and sisters.

Most chicks are born from eggs with white or brown eggshells.

I hatched from a beautiful blue egg.

Blue eggshells are very rare!

When my brothers and sisters and I were born, we all had the same soft, fluffy, puffy feathers called down.

We also had very similar voices.

We all made the sound PEEP! PEEP! PEEP!

But there was something different about me.

When my brothers and sisters were born, they could stand up right away.

When *I* was born, I was not able to stand up.

was born with something called
perosis.

Perosis means it is hard for me to stand or lift my head because one of my legs is bent.

Perosis means I have a disability.

It is hard for me to do the same things as other chicks without a little extra help.

I manage my disability by using special tools made just for me.

I wear a soft brace on my foot.

My brace keeps my toenails, or talons, from getting stuck on the floor when I walk.

I do special exercises called physical therapy.

My exercises keep the muscles in my legs strong and flexible.

Most chickens perch in high branches when they sleep.

I cannot fly, and it is hard for me to perch.

So I make a cozy nest on the ground.

My best friend in the whole world is my sister Christopher.

I'm different from Christopher because I have perosis.

She is different from me because her name is Christopher.

Some people think Christopher is an odd name for a girl.

But Christopher's name and my perosis are part of who we are, an these parts of us make us special.

Because of my perosis, I'm unable to fly or run.

Christopher is an excellent jumper, flyer, and runner.

So any time we want to see each other, she comes to me—no matter how far she has to go!

I am a lucky chick to be so loved.

I love to meet and learn about new friends.

I bet there are things about you that make you special too!